Bo and the Spooky House

by Elliott Smith
illustrated by Subi Bosa

Cicely Lewis, Executive Editor

Lerner Publications ◆ Minneapolis

A Letter from Cicely Lewis

Dear Reader,
   This series is about a boy named Bo and his grandfather in the barbershop called the Buzz. The barbershop has always been the hub of the Black community. In a world  where Black voices are often silenced, it is a place where these voices can be heard.

   I created the Read Woke challenge for my students so they can read books that reflect the diversity of the world. I hope you see the real-life beauty, richness, and joy of Black culture shine through these pages.

                    —Cicely Lewis, Executive Editor

TABLE OF CONTENTS

Bo's World

Hi, I'm Bo. I like basketball,
science, and flying in airplanes.
This is my grandpa, Roger.
I call him Pop-Pop.

We live upstairs from the Buzz. It's the barbershop Pop-Pop owns.

I like hanging out with my friends Silas, Shawn, and Zuri.

CHAPTER 1
The Dare

It was Saturday, and Bo was walking through the neighborhood with his friends. Suddenly, Shawn stopped. "Bo, I dare you to ring that doorbell," he said.

Bo looked over. They were standing next to the spooky house! Bo always walked as fast as he could past it. Overgrown plants and grass cast shadows over the house. The curtains were always closed. No one ever saw who lived there.

"I heard that house is haunted," Zuri said.

Silas shuddered. "My brother told me a scary clown lives there."

"You're not a scaredy-cat, are you, Bo?" Shawn said.

Bo cleared this throat. "Uh, no, I'm not scared. It's just a house."

Bo opened the gate. The creaking sound made his friends cover their ears. Bo waded through the tall grass.

The steps groaned as he walked up. Bo *was* scared. But he was going to prove Shawn wrong. He reached out to ring the bell.

Then, out of the corner of his eye, Bo saw a flash of something. Someone—or something—had moved the curtains inside the house!

Bo took off running. He blew past his friends and headed home.

CHAPTER 2
What's Inside?

Bo's hands shook as he folded towels in the Buzz. He was still thinking about the spooky house. The door opened, and Mr. Joe came inside. He was one of the oldest people Bo knew. Bo had an idea.

"Mr. Joe, Pop-Pop, do you know the gray house on Spring Street?" Bo asked. "My friends say it's haunted."

Mr. Joe and Pop-Pop laughed. "There's no such thing as a haunted house," Pop-Pop said.

"Mrs. Carter lives there," Mr. Joe said. "She used to be a big part of the neighborhood. But we haven't seen her much since her husband died."

"Sometimes people get real sad," Pop-Pop said to Bo.

16

Bo told the men about the dare and how he was too scared to ring the doorbell. He left out the part about running home.

"There's nothing to be scared of," Pop-Pop said with a smile. "Mrs. Carter is a nice woman."

Bo felt embarrassed. "Maybe I could go visit her," he said. Pop-Pop patted Bo on the shoulder.

"If you do, tell her to come out to church," Mr. Joe said. "And to bring some of her world-famous chocolate chip cookies!"

CHAPTER 3
Not So Scary

The next day, Bo cautiously made his way up the creaky stairs of the spooky house. He reminded himself there was nothing to be scared of. He rang the doorbell.

The door opened slowly. Bo prepared for a scary clown. Instead, he saw a woman. She smiled when she saw Bo.

"Hello, son," Mrs. Carter said. "Weren't you on my porch yesterday?"

"Uh, maybe," Bo said. "I just wanted to come say hi. My Pop-Pop owns the Buzz. He said you might like some company."

"Oh, you're Roger's grandbaby," she said. "Come on in. I just finished baking some cookies."

Bo entered to find a nice, neat house. The walls were filled with pictures. Mrs. Carter told him stories about the neighborhood and Pop-Pop. And her cookies were delicious.

The next day at school, Bo told his friends about his visit with Mrs. Carter.

"This weekend, let's help her clean up her yard," Bo said. "She said it's too hard to do by herself."

During the week, Bo asked some of the Buzz customers who knew Mrs. Carter to help too.

That weekend, half the neighborhood showed up. Mrs. Carter came outside wearing her Sunday best. She had baked cookies for everyone!

"Thank you all so much for helping me," she said.

"No problem," Bo said. "That's what friends are for."

About the Author

Elliott Smith has been writing stories ever since he was a kid. This love of writing led him first to a career as a sports reporter. Now, he has written more than 40 children's books, both fiction and nonfiction. Smith lives just outside Washington, DC, with his wife and two children. He loves watching movies, playing basketball with his kids, and adding to his collection of Pittsburgh Steelers memorabilia.

About the Illustrator

As a child, Subi Bosa drew pictures all the time, in every room of the house—sometimes on the walls. His mother still tells everyone, "He knew how to draw before he could properly hold a pencil."

In 2020, Subi was awarded a Mo Siewcharran Prize for Illustration. Subi lives in Cape Town, South Africa, creating picture books, comics, and graphic novels.

Lerner Publications Company
An imprint of Lerner Publishing Group, Inc.
241 First Avenue North
Minneapolis, MN 55401 USA

For reading levels and more information, look up this title at www.lernerbooks.com.

Main body text set in Mikado 24/41. Typeface provided by Hannes von Doehren.

Library of Congress Cataloging-in-Publication Data

Names: Smith, Elliott, 1976- author. | Bosa, Subi, illustrator.
Title: Bo and the spooky house / by Elliott Smith ; illustrated by Subi Bosa.
Description: Minneapolis : Lerner Publications, [2023] | Series: Bo at the Buzz
    (Read woke chapter books) | Audience: Ages 6–9. | Audience: Grades 2–3. |
    Summary: When Bo decides to ring the doorbell of the spooky house on Spring
    Street, he does not expect to discover an opportunity to learn about treating
    neighbors with kindness and friendship.
Identifiers: LCCN 2022011638 (print) | LCCN 2022011639
    (ebook) | ISBN 9781728476155 (lib. bdg.) | ISBN 9781728486291 (pbk.) |
    ISBN 9781728481555 (eb pdf)
Subjects: CYAC: Neighborliness—Fiction. | African Americans—Fiction.
Classification: LCC PZ7.1.S626 Bos 2023 (print) | LCC PZ7.1.S626 (ebook) | DDC
    [Fic]—dc23

LC record available at https://lccn.loc.gov/2022011638
LC ebook record available at https://lccn.loc.gov/2022011639

Manufactured in the United States of America
2-1009304-50645-3/15/2023